ISBN 978-1-0686176-0-7

Cassie Wilson

The Compound Cats

Deep within the woodlands was a magical place.

Every day thousands of excited people arrived to have fun with their friends, family, or just to have some peaceful alone time.

There were so many things to do!

Eating tasty treats, riding rides and wonderful walks through mystical gardens.

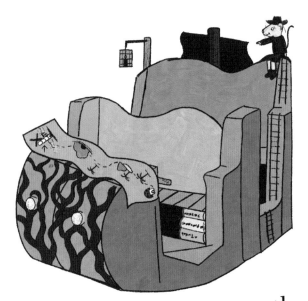

Not to forget
the waterparks to splash around in,
and the hotels to snooze in after a long day.

But our story today isn't about these people.

Down,

down,

down...

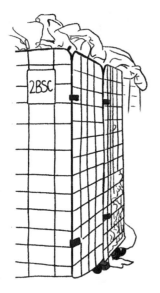

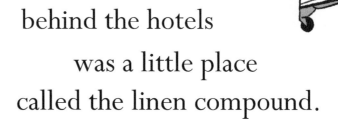

behind the hotels
was a little place
called the linen compound.

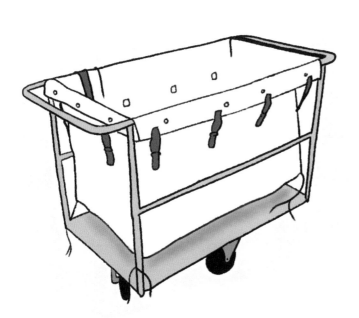

This is where all of the clean linen arrived
and the dirty linen went ready to be washed.
But down in the compound, secretly,
there lived a family of...

CATS!

Behind the trolleys and cages,
keeping herself out of sight,
lived a mummy cat called Soapy,
who's fur was silky and white.

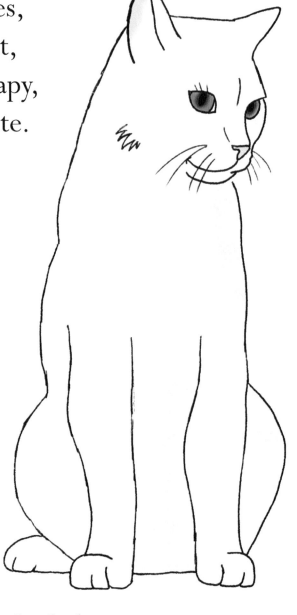

Soapy had four little kittens,
who were full of mischief and fun.
They loved nothing more
than to play and explore,
to jump, to pounce, and to run.

Each day they would explore this magical place,
unsure of what it really was.

Their mother warned them that they should stay hidden,
and never go near any of the mysterious things
that had appeared over the years.

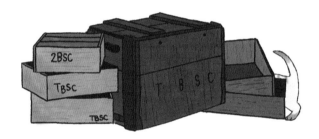

The kittens listened to their mother,
and watched from nearby trees or bushes.

Kitten number one was called Huss.

He loved to run fast everywhere.

Huss was brave and liked to try new things.

He enjoyed being up in the air!

Huss had a few favourite spots in the park

where he watched all of the people laugh and scream.

He imagined how it must feel to fly.

To leap that far and fast was his dream.

One day he witnessed something brand new.
Lots of people with hard hats and cranes,
were dropping in a giant steel monster.
It was more than he could explain!

He imagined his own giant monster,

which would give out a wondrous   ROAR!

He envisioned the chains, and the banks, and the dives.

Spins, loops, and launches galore.

The second kitten they liked to call Splash.

Can you guess where she liked to play?

Thats right!

Splash was an unusual cat.

She searched for water everyday!

Some days she would cross over the car park,

and watch through the gates and the trees.

The fountains sprayed high up in the air,

as she caught a feel of the mist in the breeze.

She slept on top of the waterslides,
    and listened to the water rushing through.

She loved to bound through the puddles.
    Splash dreamed that she could slide too.

In the park, she would marvel at waterfalls

sending people and boats spinning around.

She watched the pirates spraying their water cannons,

as children ducked
down to the ground.

On to the third little kitten called Talbot,
who was much more calm and reserved.
He enjoyed taking morning strolls through the gardens,
and chatting away to the birds.

The gardens were tranquil and peaceful.
He could think and dream all day.
He could learn about the flora and monuments
put there by a man who added colour to grey.

There was a dog on the wall that spat water,

which Talbot found rather odd.

There were arches,
and domes,
and big glass windows!

Stories of sadness and love.

Talbot dreamed of the day when,

he could build a spectacular design of his own.

Maybe a castle with chimneys and slides!

A perfect place to call home.

The final kitten was called Mack.

She had an imagination that was sure to impress.

She watched in wonder and amazement.

It was the dark rides that she liked the best!

She imagined stories of whimsy and fun.
Tales of monsters and ghouls.
Tunnels, lights, sounds and effects.
Magical themes and interesting vehicles.

She imagined the stories these places would tell.
Poor Mack never got to see inside.
She would sit and wonder for hours each day,
and watch as the pieces arrived.

Back at the compound she made her own magic.
All of her siblings joined too.
She would tell them tales of whimsical worlds,
and their ideas grew and grew.

At night they got comfy in the linen but in the winter
things got cold, and the shelter sometimes leaked.

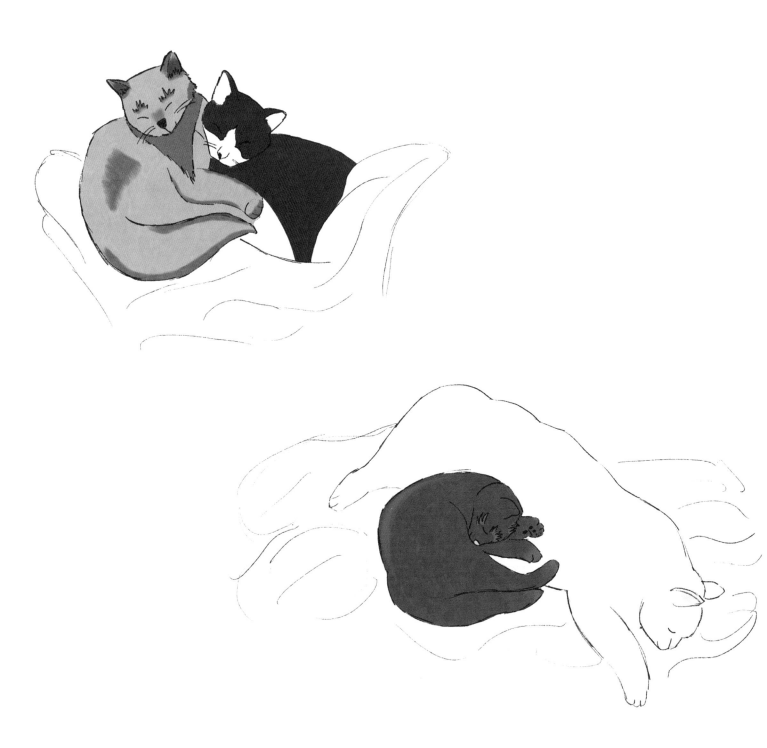

The compound cats snuggled together and tried to stay warm.
But mama cat worried about her little kittens.

After the snow fell heavily one night, mama explained
to them that it might be best if they found
homes with humans for the winter time.

So the next day, the compound cats followed the
workers and made themselves known.

In a few days, Huss, Splash, Mack
and Talbot all found homes with
loving humans.

Mama cat hid in her usual spots. She was missing her kittens terribly, but she felt happy that they were safe.

She wondered if she would see them again.

But as the spring began to bloom, and the people began to arrive again in their thousands...

One wonderful night…

She did!

They all laughed, and played, and snuggled together again.

What a magical season it was.

Printed in Great Britain
by Amazon

41774825R00016